LORETTA KRUPINSKI

PIRATE TREASURE

DUTTON CHILDREN'S BOOKS

"Some are weatherwise, some are otherwise."

—BENJAMIN FRANKLIN

DUTTON CHILDREN'S BOOKS
A division of Penguin Young Readers Group
Published by the Penguin Group • Penguin Group (USA) Inc., 375 Hudson Street, New York, New York 10014, U.S.A.
Penguin Group (Canada), 90 Eglinton Avenue East, Suite 700, Toronto, Ontario, Canada M4P 2Y3 (a division of Pearson Penguin Canada Inc.)
Penguin Books Ltd, 80 Strand, London WC2R 0RL, England
Penguin Ireland, 25 St Stephen's Green, Dublin 2, Ireland (a division of Penguin Books Ltd)
Penguin Group (Australia), 250 Camberwell Road, Camberwell, Victoria 3124, Australia (a division of Pearson Australia Group Pty Ltd)
Penguin Books India Pvt Ltd, 11 Community Centre, Panchsheel Park, New Delhi - 110 017, India
Penguin Group (NZ), Cnr Airborne and Rosedale Roads, Albany, Auckland 1310, New Zealand (a division of Pearson New Zealand Ltd)
Penguin Books (South Africa) (Pty) Ltd, 24 Sturdee Avenue, Rosebank, Johannesburg 2196, South Africa
Penguin Books Ltd, Registered Offices: 80 Strand, London WC2R 0RL, England

Library of Congress Cataloging-in-Publication Data

Krupinski, Loretta.
Pirate treasure / by Loretta Krupinski.—1st ed.
p. cm.
Summary: When pirates Captain Oliver and Rosie decide to try farming near the town of Mousam
they learn that the sayings about weather that they used while at sea are equally useful on land.
ISBN 0-525-47579-6
[1. Pirates—Fiction. 2. Weather—Fiction. 3. Mice—Fiction. 4. Farm life—Fiction.] I. Title.
PZ7.K94624Pir 2006
[E]—dc22
2005004796

Published in the United States by Dutton Children's Books,
a division of Penguin Young Readers Group
345 Hudson Street, New York, New York 10014
www.penguin.com/youngreaders

Designed by Irene Vandervoort

Manufactured in China   First Edition

1 3 5 7 9 10 8 6 4 2

A furious storm rode in on a northeast wind. When it was over, the pirate ship *Daisy* had been driven up a river.

Captain Oliver steered the vessel behind an island. There was damage to the rigging, sails were torn, and the ship leaked.

"Look lively, Rosie. Let go the anchor," said the captain.

"I was scared," said Rosie.

Me, too, thought the captain.

Seagulls huddled at the edge of the water, seeking shelter from the storm at sea. The captain saw them and said, "Seagull, seagull, stay on the sand—it's never good weather when you are inland." And it wasn't. The storm had come so suddenly, the captain was not prepared.

"Rosie, it's very important to be alert to changes in the weather. If you expect bad weather, then you can stay safe and dry."

"Aye, I know that," said Rosie.

"Our ship needs repair, so let's scuttle our plans to raid the warehouses for grain. We can explore the river instead. Maybe there be treasure here," said the captain.

The sun set that evening in a sky so pretty it looked as if the storm had never happened. Gazing at the red sky, he said, "Good weather it will be. We will sail in the morning. Red sky at night, sailors delight. Red sky in the morning, sailors take warning."

"Aye, I know that," said Rosie with a sigh.

Past Rattling Stones Beach, the river narrowed and the waters ran smooth. The trees spread out on either side, crowding the shore. Much like a house, the leaves grew into walls and became a green roof overhead.

They continued sailing upriver, past a tiny village under a large, gnarly beech tree. Farther upstream, Captain Oliver lowered the sails and dropped anchor. "No weather is ill if the wind be still," he said with a sigh.

"Aye, I know that," said Rosie.

Under the light of a rising moon, they went belowdecks and slept, tired but anxious to begin a new adventure.

Captain Oliver awoke to see a field of rippling grass that reminded him of waves.

"It's pleasant and peaceful here, Rosie," he said.

Rosie agreed. "That last storm was very scary," she said. "Why don't we stay? We can live on the ship. We can grow our own corn and grain."

The captain said thoughtfully, "There be a lot I don't know about farming, but by summer's end, I'll make the *Daisy* good as new. Aye, let's plant our fortune here." Together they hauled the *Daisy* up on the beach to repair the leaks.

The next morning, they awoke to bird songs. A veil of vapors hung over the water. The captain called down to Rosie, "It's going to be a nice day. When the mist comes in from the sea, then good weather it will be."

"Aye, I know that," she called up.

"You stand watch, Rosie," the captain called out, breaking the still water into ripples with his oars. "I'm heading downstream to the village."

As he rowed closer, the captain saw a sign nailed to the beech tree that said MOUSAM VILLAGE.

"Ahoy, mateys," he said, stowing his dinghy. "I've come upriver on the good ship *Daisy*, and I will need supplies. Look lively now—where can I find tools, nails, and rope for rigging?"

The villagers gathered round. Some of the younger ones giggled. "Why is he dressed so funny?" a little one asked.

The villagers pointed to the door inside the tree. Food and hardware lined the shelves. The clerk brought out nails and rope. Captain Oliver said, "I'm going to grow my own corn and grain, and I will need a shovel, a rake, and a hoe, too. I'll take a sack of grain, some dried apple rings, a package of these blue flower seeds, and a new hat for me Rosie."

The clerk said, "I guess you'll be needing a pair of overalls, too. No one farms in a sash, if you don't mind my saying so." Trying not to laugh, the clerk also suggested replacing the captain's funny-looking hat with a straw one.

Back outside, the captain looked up at the sky. "Weather is important to know, whether you are at sea or on land," he said. He pointed to the sky. "If clouds look like they were scratched by a hen, be ready to reef the sails in. You landlubbers, be sure to batten your hatches. Come upriver, me hearties, and have a gam on my ship." With that, he pushed off in his dinghy, leaving a trail of ripples in the water behind him.

"What are hatches?" someone asked.

"Is it something to do with birds' eggs?" asked another.

"What's a gam?" his friend asked.

"Do you think he's a pirate?" someone wondered. There was a gasp, and everyone fled back into their homes.

Captain Oliver worked hard to repair the *Daisy*. Rosie worked harder to make the ship into a home. Later that evening, the river folk cautiously peered through the grasses to look at the strangers and their ship. Captain Oliver and Rosie had fallen into a deep sleep down below and never knew they were there.

When he wasn't repairing the ship, the captain helped Rosie in the garden. In his new overalls and hat, Captain Oliver tilled the soil. Rosie raked it smooth. The seeds were planted, along with much hope. In spite of too much rain or not enough, the seeds soon began to sprout. Captain Oliver and Rosie were very proud of themselves.

One day, the captain saw beady brown eyes peering back at him through the leaves in the vegetable garden.

"Blast those crows! Blast those groundhogs! Blast those rabbits! Those pillaging pests are eating our crops!" he yelled.

"Oh, no, look at this!" cried Rosie, picking beetles off the squash plants. "What shall we do?"

"Belay those tears, Rosie," said the captain. "We will scare them off with my old clothes. They will think it's really me instead."

The scarecrow kept the crows from eating the new corn, but the groundhogs and rabbits were not fooled, and those beady brown eyes glistened in the shadows.

Captain Oliver stooped down, put another beetle in the bucket, and said, "It's easier to live at sea, isn't it, me Rosie?"

"Aye, I know that, but I like it here," she said.

Twittering and laughter came from behind them. They caught sight of some of the villagers running off through the rows of corn.

It was a fine summer day, with the sky especially blue and scattered with clouds, when Captain Oliver said, "Look lively now. When mountains and cliffs appear, a lot of showers and rain are near."

"Aye, I know that," said Rosie.

Captain Oliver grew even more alert as he watched bigger mountains and bigger cliffs appear in the clouds. A capful of wind became a gale. Showers turned to torrents of rain.

"Get below, Rosie. The water is rising," the captain cried out. The good ship *Daisy* was afloat again.

"Shiver me timbers!" the captain cried out suddenly. "We must sail to the village!" He hoisted the newly patched sails, hauled up the anchor, and let the floodwaters take them downriver to Mousam.

The villagers saw the captain's ship on the rising water. "Please save us!" they called from the tree branches.

The captain threw lines from fore and aft to some of the villagers. "Hold on to those lines, you swabs, until we get everyone on board!" he called out while helping women and children off the tree and onto the deck. "Rosie, take the little ones below!" he ordered.

"Look lively now! I'll raise the sails, and you there—cast off the bowline! We'll head for a cove."

The waves were high, and the wind whistled through the new rigging.
"Blow me down! I feel like I'm back at sea again!" the captain called out.
"Remember this, you landlubbers: The sharper the blast, the sooner it's past."

At last the storm moved on. The riverbanks rose up as the water level went down. Now that the weather was calm, the villagers were more talkative.

"This sure is a nice ship, Captain Oliver," said one.

"Thank you for saving us," said another. "We never would have made it without your ship."

"He's not such a bad guy after all," Rosie heard someone else say.

"Can we go sailing again?" a little one asked.

"Aye, aye," said the captain, beaming.

Rosie and the captain sailed back to their garden and dropped anchor. Their crops and flowers were flattened to the ground.

"Our grain is ruined," said the captain. "Our treasure is gone."

"We still have our home, and now we have friends, too. Why don't we try again?" said Rosie.

"And scuttle me plans?" said the captain.

"Aye, aye," said Rosie with a smile.

The river folk soon rebuilt what was destroyed by the flood, and everything was the same as it was before—except for one thing. Captain Oliver was now a hero in Mousam. He began teaching the villagers about weather and how it could affect their land. They shared their seeds and grain and taught him about farming.

Captain Oliver said to Rosie, "The real treasure in life is not found in gold or grain, but in our friends."

"Didn't you know that?" said Rosie, smiling.

Seagull, seagull, stay on the sand—it's never
good weather when you are inland.

Red sky at night, sailors delight.
Red sky in the morning, sailors take warning.

No weather is ill if the wind be still.

When the mist comes in from the sea,
then good weather it will be.

If clouds look like they were scratched by a hen,
be ready to reef the sails in.

When mountains and cliffs appear,
a lot of showers and rain are near.

The sharper the blast, the sooner it's past.